DANGER IN THE CANYON

A Western Novella

A.T. BUTLER

CHAPTER ONE

Jacob Payne dismounted. The scorching Arizona sun beat relentlessly down, drenching his dark, close-cropped hair with sweat and plastering it to his skull. With one hand he took off his hat to fan his face, and with the other took hold of the reins to lead his pinto down through the uneven, rocky bank of the dry riverbed. The sandy ground shifted and crumbled under his feet.

As he took the first step through the brush, the dirt bank collapsed and one of the ragweed plants uprooted altogether. Jacob almost lost his balance as he slipped down the low slope. Even a desert plant couldn't hang on forever without water, and Jacob knew he would be the same way. A body could only take so much.

The tall man paused to let the dirt and rocks tumble down the rest of the bank while he replaced his hat. His shirt clung to his sides, tight across his broad shoulders, the sweat running down his back under the layers. He blinked back the sweat dripping into his eyes. Once the rocks had settled he would lead his horse across, searching again for both water and his man. He couldn't risk his horse making a false step. He couldn't risk sweating out all his water. He still had a ways to go.

The bounty hunter had been on the outlaw's trail for three days now, winding away from Tucson, far to the south and the west, following his mark. While he thought he had packed enough water when he set out, the canteen was already running dangerously low. He had been able to supplement a little along the way, but if he didn't find a substantial source of water soon he might have to give up this hunt.

Jacob had never walked away from a reward once he began tracking, and he had no intention of starting now. The man he was after would need water just as badly, and Jacob knew he could best him.

Jacob led the pinto down the final few crumbling steps to the riverbed. Sparse, hardy desert weeds and animal burrows were beginning to crop up in the middle of the dry plane, life continuing in the absence of running water. After a few feet, the dry, cracked dirt revealed the faint impression of a pair of horseshoes. Jacob squatted down and compared them to the depth of his own print. Judging from how much dust had been blown away, he guessed he was standing right where Jed Corker had crossed less than one day past.

He stood again, looking for further prints, eyeing the horizon, and considering his options. Jacob paused to swallow a mouthful of water from his canteen.

Before he'd left town, several long-time locals had warned Jacob about the monsoon they expected any day, pressing him to take an extra coil of rope and more jerky than he had packed. "You'll not be able to see your own hand," they had said. "You've not seen a storm of this like." He had not yet been in such a squall here in Arizona, but he'd heard tell of torrential storms that could appear as though out of nowhere, dumping gallons of water in only an hour, or of a wall of dust sweeping across the territory, obscuring every living thing in its path.

But Jacob had been in storms before; this didn't concern him none. He packed his saddlebags, filled his canteen, and didn't fret. When he had left Virginia almost a year ago to come west, he'd thought he was escaping the wet and the humidity. The fierce heat of the Arizona desert was like a balm, and for the last few months he felt like he was truly dry for the first time in his life.

Such scorching drought, he knew, would only be bearable for as long as he had water to drink. He'd gotten used to recognizing signs that he needed more water, since he'd taken to spending so much time in the desert. A monsoon would give him all the water he could want, but he couldn't count on that storm finding him. He had been rationing as well as he could, but Jacob would need to find other sources if he was going to make his way back.

Standing in the middle of the riverbed, Jacob scanned the horizon ahead of him. In this midday heat, most of the desert animals would be resting deep underground. Without a lick of wind to stir the shrubs, Jacob heard only his own breathing. Wherever Corker had got to, he was not within hearing distance.

About a mile or two on up, small hills rose

and so did Jacob's hopes. He squinted his eyes against the sun and made out some low mesquite trees and what looked like a canyon extending between the hills. From this distance, it was impossible to tell how wide or deep the canyon was, but there was an unmistakable shady area beckoning to him. He'd have to keep an eye out for prints, but a cool hole like that would be where Corker would head to. Shade, maybe even water. Trees meant there must be some kind of dampness, at least.

Jacob grinned to himself. Unless he was much mistaken about the other man's desire for survival, he expected to find his target and make his arrest that afternoon—maybe even within the hour.

"Well, Paint," Jacob said as he poured water into the palm of his wide hand and offered it to the horse. "What do you think? Seems Corker is probably up there waiting for us, huh? Ready to keep going?"

The horse lapped up the water eagerly and nuzzled Jacob's ear. The bounty hunter nodded, took hold of the reins, and continued leading his companion through the arid terrain.

CHAPTER TWO

Three days earlier, before setting off into the desert, Jacob had been eating supper at San Xavier Cafe in Tucson, his favorite meal when in town. The locals were friendly, and Bonnie, who brought meals most nights, always had a coy smile for him. He had helped some of her unwanted suitors find the door more than once, and she had yet to stop thanking him.

By the front door, Bobby played a lively tune on the piano, humming under his breath while the cafe filled with regulars. Edwin Hogg caught Jacob's eye with a grin as he crossed the threshold. He'd be wantin' a hand or three of poker, no doubt, Jacob thought. He took another bite. Jackrabbit stew and coffee filled Jacob's stomach while he contemplated his next move.

The U.S. Marshal's office down the street had a stack of wanted posters nearly two feet high, and all Jacob had to do was pick one. The number of degenerate men pouring west into Arizona meant Jacob would be kept busy. Men who had not been able to find their place after the war ended. Men who already had murders or thefts on their conscience and came out to the open desert where they thought they could get away with more. Jacob had come to the cafe for supper, yes, but also for information. If anyone in town had even a hint of where one of these outlaws was at, Jacob would follow the trail without a second thought.

Jacob had just asked Bonnie for a second cup of coffee and more cornbread when one of the town's deputies burst through the door, yanked his hat from his head, and pitched it across the room at an empty table.

"Blast!" Deputy Lowry exclaimed, stomping after his hat.

He followed that outburst by kicking over the closest empty chair, causing the two women seated at that table to gasp in surprise.

The deputy stomped off after his hat, sinking down into the chair at the table in the corner, alone, and crossing his arms across his chest, chewing furiously.

"What seems to be the problem, deputy?" Jacob asked after him. "Somethin' happen?"

He stood to right the chair and apologize to the poor surprised women. They both held hands over their chests as though trying to still their beating hearts, looking askance at the fuming deputy.

"Damn straight, somethin' happened!" He turned his head and spat a straight stream of tobacco juice into the spittoon by the wall behind him. "Jed Corker escaped."

Jacob took his now-full cup of coffee from his original seat and sat down across from Deputy Lowry in his corner table. "Corker? Ain't he with the Slippery Stone Gang?"

"He is. Or was. It's none too clear. He held up the Valleseco Bank on his own, with no help from Stone or anyone else in the gang. Just a couple days ago, this was. Managed to kill two tellers who didn't move fast enough for his liking and wound a woman, one of the bank's customers. Violence ain't Stone's way. I don't know that he's ever killed an innocent. My guess is Corker's out on his ear and desperate to make do."

"But you caught him, didn't ya?"

"We did. Deputy Little'n me caught up with him not far outside of town and was bringing him back to stand trial when he slipped away from us."

"How'd that happen?"

"No tellin'. Elliott 'Slippery' Stone must've taught him a trick or two. Woke up this morning and he was gone. Stole a horse, but he left his take from Valleseco Bank. Me'n Deputy Little raced back here to send the telegrams out to nearby towns. Wayne City and Solano both have banks less than a day's ride from here. If Corker's feelin' desperate, he might try again."

Jacob nodded darkly. "There's nothing more vicious than a desperate man."

Lowry spat again. "I don't like it one bit."

Jacob stood up.

"Tell me exactly where you lost him. I can pick up the trail."

Deputy Lowry remained in his seat and leaned back to put his boots on the table. A fine layer of dust shook loose and coated the wooden surface. "Now, look, Payne. Corker is a dangerous creature, and the Valleseco bank ain't offered a bounty of any kind. I don't want you to go gettin' yourself killed for nothing."

Jacob took one last swig of the bitter black coffee before setting the mug down on the table. The heat and the adrenaline of the hunt coursed through his limbs. Edwin and his card game could wait.

"Beggin' your pardon, deputy, but the man killed two people, wounded more, and could be on his way to do more damage. If I can stop him, I will. Reward or no reward. Tell me where you lost him."

Once he had wrung all the details he could from Deputy Lowry, it took Jacob less than an hour to claim his horse from the livery, stock up on his water and supplies, and hit the road, south and west into the desert.

CHAPTER THREE

Now, three days on the trail, Jacob was mad as a hornet and even more determined to get his man. He had followed the bank robber through flat terrain, around low hills, and between two small silver mines. Jacob all but lost the trail a couple times where miners' carts and mules' hoofprints obscured the track. Corker must have known he was being tailed; he'd tried to lose Jacob near the abandoned Espejo mine, covering his tracks and attempting misdirection. Once, Jacob had got close enough that the man had left his campfire burning in his haste to escape, but Jacob had just missed him.

Only once before had a wanted man eluded him so long, but Jacob didn't think this Corker fella was anything special.

Once he and Paint had climbed out of the riverbed up the opposite bank, Jacob mounted again. He nudged the horse forward, but it stepped sideways around the mouth of a burrow that the bounty hunter hadn't noticed, half hidden by the brittlebush overgrowth.

"Good job, boy," Jacob murmured to his mount. "You're smarter than me sometimes."

From his vantage atop the pinto, Jacob could see that the river curved around to the north of him. There was a small concentration of agave plants along the riverbed, extending about fifty feet to his left and curving back toward the hills where Jacob was heading. That was a good sign. Chances he'd find water in that canyon were much stronger if a river sometimes ran from it.

Jacob's mouth felt dry, and he was having trouble swallowing. He pulled out his canteen again and allowed himself a more full drink, coming closer to quenching his thirst yet still missing the mark. He drank again. He sensed he was close to the final confrontation with Corker and wanted to be ready. Full strength. Leave nothing to chance.

Jacob sat high above the flat terrain, in full view of anyone who might be watching. He held no hope of ambushing or surprising the outlaw. The man would be watching for him, no doubt, readying his gun or knife. Jacob's only course would be to overpower the man. He would like to be able to take him alive, but he knew that it might not be possible to walk away with both his own life and Corker's still intact.

He unhooked his hammer loop and pulled his revolver free, resting it carefully in one hand while he held the horse's reins with the other. Another quick nudge and Paint began walking forward, around the brittlebush and to the shady canyon up ahead. Jacob kept it slow; he needed to keep all his focus on the mouth of the canyon, eyes peeled for movement or activ-ity, and let the horse take watch for animals and danger below.

Ten, twenty, forty feet through the brush, Paint brought Jacob closer to his target. He felt a rivulet of sweat running down the back of his head to his collar. At about twenty yards from the canyon, Jacob pulled back, pausing Paint's advance. He took a deep breath, breathing in through his nose and filling his lungs. The bounty hunter had always had a keen sense of smell, and he found that paying attention to slight variations in the air helped him more oft than not. There was a heavy, smoky touch woven into the dirt and light floral ahead.

A campfire, Jacob thought. Maybe he's cooking, or maybe he just put it out from this morning, but I smell wood burning.

He bent forward, close to the horse's mane, and looked again. No sign of movement up ahead, but that smell was an unmistakable sign.

"Once we get to the cool of that canyon, we'll rest, pal," Jacob promised, again nudging the horse forward. "We've got him cornered."

Jacob stopped again just five yards from the mouth of the canyon. The smell of burnt wood was even stronger here, and it didn't take him long to spot the source. Just to the right of the path was a small, still smoldering campfire.

Jacob eyed it with suspicion.

Why would anyone be burning a fire this late in the day, especially if that person was trying to stay hid? And why would someone on the run build a fire in such plain sight in the first place? The outlaw had already demonstrated he knew Jacob was following him; this campfire could be a trap, an ambush, or a distraction.

And Jacob wasn't aiming to get caught unawares.

Jacob pulled his eyes from the embers and scanned the interior of the canyon. About fifteen yards from the mouth, the walls began to get steep and almost vertical, and between here and there were taller bushes and even a couple trees. Harsh shadows stretched across the ground, and Jacob looked hard for evidence of another human being.

A tiny flash of light caught Jacob's eye. He turned Paint back around toward the mouth of the canyon and realized it was the glint of sun on steel.

"That you, Corker? You wanna make this easy or hard?"

Paint turned in a full circle, stepping around a barrel cactus, and Jacob lost sight of the steel barrel of the gun as he turned. If the outlaw was hiding out in this canyon, they both knew it was only a matter of time before Jacob would catch up with him.

"Corker!" he called again as he nudged Paint forward.

"Don't come any closer," a deep, gravely voice warned.

With the echo within the canyon walls, Jacob couldn't quite place where that voice was coming from. No further wink of gun showed in the sun.

"Give up, Corker," Jacob called. "I don't want to have to kill you."

A loud, hearty laugh answered him. "I warned you . . ." the stranger said, his voice trailing off. "You'll not be the one doing the killing."

Jacob leaned down to pet Paint's shoulder. "We got him, boy. Let's go."

The horse had only taken two more steps toward the canyon when Jacob heard the crack of gunfire, followed closely by the whinny of the pinto in pain. Before he could take another breath, he felt the animal collapse underneath him, falling, crumbling to the ground.

CHAPTER FOUR

"Corker!" Jacob yelled into the canyon. His voice echoed and bounced off the rock, but he could still hear the rustle and crash of a man running through the wilderness. "You devil!"

His right leg was pinned under Paint, who lay on his side whimpering. Jacob didn't think his leg was any worse hurt than bruised, but the horse wouldn't be able to recover from that fatal blast.

The outlaw had shot the horse in his right shoulder, dropping the poor animal to the ground with Jacob still on top. Now footsteps raced away, echoing around the canyon. Jacob cursed under his breath—his mark was escaping . . . but he had to deal with the situation at hand first.

Jacob slowly, carefully, maneuvered his foot out from under the injured horse. The width of his boot was still wrapped in his stirrup. He had to twist his ankle to disentangle himself, driving the toe of his boot into the horse's ribs. Jacob cursed under his breath again, going slowly and trying not to hurt Paint any further.

He squatted before the horse, examining the wound where the bullet had embedded in the heavy muscle. Blood rivulets were already trailing down to the dust underneath the creature.

"Shhh . . ." Jacob whispered as he held his revolver to the horse's head. "I'm sorry, boy."

The horse whinnied again and Jacob's heart sank. Paint had been his companion ever since he left Texas and crossed over to the Arizona Territory, and he had hoped they'd still have years left together. The animal had helped him track and catch up with at least half of the outlaws Jacob had put in shackles. The poor beast deserved better than this death, alone in the dust and blood at the mouth of a nameless canyon.

Jacob closed his eyes as he squeezed the trigger. The crack of gunshot echoed through the canyon, and the horse's whinnies abruptly ceased.

After letting out a long, deep sigh, Jacob set to work rescuing his saddle, bags, canteen, and bedroll from Paint's corpse. He was three days' ride out from the closest town—how long would that be on foot? He shook the canteen. The contents sloshed around in the bottom of the leather container. Jacob estimated less than a quarter full. Enough for the rest of the day, but no longer.

Well, he thought with a sigh. At least he wouldn't need to share the water with Paint anymore.

When he was done, a pile of his necessities sat to the side of the path. What would he need to take with him as he proceeded on foot, and what could he leave behind? Jacob looked up and judged the position of the sun in the sky. With Corker so close, he waged he could capture that man and make it back here by nightfall. He would only carry what he needed to subdue the outlaw: rope, coiled tightly and slung over his shoulder; two revolvers, each with a bullet ready in the chamber; canteen of water, for when he found the spring he prayed would be back there; and a Bowie knife, tucked in his boot just in case.

As Jacob stood, still some yards from the mouth of the canyon, he felt exposed on the flat horizon. His gaze raked the shaded space between the hills, looking for any further sign of Corker, but found nothing. The man had already run deeper into the canyon.

Jacob began his cautious advance.

He walked past the smoldering campfire at the mouth of the canyon without giving it a second glance. There were no other signs or indications that a camp of any kind had been made here. Instead, Corker had apparently set up this small burning wood as a trap—a trap Jacob and Paint had walked right into. It was easy bait to lure in any lawman who might be following him and looking for signs of him. He'd then waited for his chance to incapacitate his pursuer.

Wherever Corker had gone, Jacob no longer heard him. No echo of footsteps or rumble of laughter reached his ears. He paused in the shade of a mesquite tree and readjusted his rope over his shoulder, then hiked up into the depths of the canyon.

It was another thirty feet into the canyon

before Jacob noticed any other signs of the outlaw. It was easy to miss, but he spotted a set of footprints and the butt of a barely smoked cigarette down behind the large rocks jutting out of the side of the canyon wall. Jacob squatted down to take a closer look; judging from the print, it looked like Corker had also been squatting there on the balls of his feet, probably just waiting and watching for whatever lawman was on his trail.

Jacob smiled grimly to himself, pleased that he had so disturbed the other man's escape plans. The more Corker worried about what the bounty hunter was doing, the more chance there would be that he would slip up and make a mistake. Just judging from the man's errors so far, Jacob knew it was only a matter of time before he could push his clear-headed, even-keeled, patient advantage.

The cigarette still smoldered, so Jacob ground it into the dirt under his heel. There were many reasons Jacob didn't smoke; the fact that the dregs could give away his location was just one of them.

Corker's bootprints sprinted deeper into the canyon. Jacob sped up his tracking, following the clear path of Corker's down the middle of the ravine to where it turned around a bend on the right.

The canyon walls towered high above Jacob's head, forty feet above him and blocking out the sun. Ahead of him, the ravine curved to the right, parallel to Corker's footprints.

Jacob hurried his steps. Walking through the shade between the two hills immediately gave Jacob more energy, as short a respite it may be. He hadn't minded being in the direct sun for so long, but now that he was out of it, he could move faster and work harder without as much of a danger of losing all his water. Here, where the ground was still mostly even, where the dry riverbed transitioned into the level ground of the canyon, Jacob could almost set off at a run.

He turned the corner. The prints disappeared and the canyon broke into three separate paths.

Jacob paused, unsure of how to proceed.

CHAPTER FIVE

Three branches. Three choices. Three chances to be wrong in his guess where Jed Corker had got to.

Jacob took only a quick glance before choosing the middle path. The path on the left was dappled in cool shade from the trees; the path on the right was wide and bright, almost welcoming in its stillness. But the path in the middle was the darkest, the shadiest, and the narrowest. It was the most likely to dead-end, but also possibly the most likely to have more caves and corners to hide in and ambush someone from.

That's where Jacob would go if he were the man on the run.

He didn't slow his pace. Gripping the rope

over his left shoulder and his revolver in his right hand, he took long, almost bouncing strides up the path. This narrow canyon had some corners and rocks that jutted out, and it seemed to get more confined the farther he went. At times Jacob even had to turn sideways to fit his broad shoulders through the ravine. He kept his eyes open for more clues to Corker's trail, but kept moving forward.

His hurried steps and long legs helped him cover a lot of ground quickly, so it was only about ten minutes before he realized he was on the wrong path.

Jacob turned left around another bend in the canyon, only to have to stop abruptly. He had found himself at a dead end. The rock wall soared above his head, smooth and unmarked by footholds—no indication that the other man had ever been here. The bounty hunter pursed his lips, exhaling roughly in frustration. He had guessed incorrectly.

"Dammit," he cursed to himself.

Corker kept slipping out of his grasp. The outlaw had managed to increase his advantage simply through Jacob's wrong assumption.

He backtracked to where the three branches of the canyon began. Hands on hips, eyes scanning the terrain, Jacob paused, unsure of how to proceed. He was sure the outlaw's path had turned the corner into this branch of the canyon, but *then* where had he gone?

Jacob backed up a few steps to look again at the footprints. Corker's boots plainly ran up the dirt path, then stopped at the branch. He examined both walls of the ravine, looking for signs the man had climbed rather than run farther.

Not only was there no indication of anyone scaling up the rock face, but Jacob didn't even see any indication that there were foot- or handholds that would aid him in a climb up. The stone seemed moderately smoothed, worn down by centuries of water and wind coursing through this canyon. Experimentally, he tugged on the scraggly weed growing out of a crack. It easily came free of the dirt and into his hand. There were no good anchors to aid in a climb up the rock face.

Corker must have traveled deeper into the canyon on foot, but had hidden his footprints somehow.

Jacob was frustrated, flexing his hand into a fist. He took a deep breath and willed himself to think through this slowly, logically. He could sense he was close, and he just wanted to go tearing down one of the branches of the canyon to find his target, but if he chose wrong again he would have to backtrack and waste untold amounts of time.

He closed his eyes, imagining what he would do if he were Corker, how he would escape a tracker or erase the clues that pointed to his whereabouts.

Erase. That was it.

Jacob opened his eyes again and looked more carefully at the dust under his feet where the outlaw's footprints ended. There was a different quality to the ground here in the canyon than had been out in the desert or the riverbed. In fact—he looked again—there was a different quality here than was even in the first part of the canyon. It almost seemed to have brushstrokes in the dirt.

He stepped to the edge of the path, careful not to disturb the pattern on the ground, and stalked ahead, totally focused on the dirt beneath him. There was a very clear pattern of sweeping back and forth. Jacob suspected that Corker had used a branch of shrub or tree to wipe out evidence of his footprints behind him as he progressed. But here the joke fell on

Corker: the sweeping marks themselves were enough of a track for Jacob.

Once he knew what to look for, the outlaw's path was obvious. Jacob traced the erasing pattern from where the ravine turned, down toward the branch of canyon on the right, and another twenty yards, until the tree branch he had used was discarded on the side of the canyon and the bootprints resumed.

Jacob snorted, holding in his laughter. Corker was lazy. He may have learned some tricks from Elliott "Slippery" Stone on how to escape, but he wasn't as thorough or committed as he should be. That would be his downfall.

Now that he was positive he was on the correct trail, Jacob hurried his tracking again. He shook his head in wonder at Corker's choice. There was nowhere in this fork of the canyon to hide, not even any plants or boulders in this stretch. His bootprints were plain as day in the dirt floor, as though calling for Jacob to follow him.

The canyon curved slowly around to the left, where small boulders lay strewn across the path.

Jacob stepped up into the narrow path between the boulders.

A rattle arrested his next movement.

The rattle soon became two, three, and innumerable rattles echoing all about him. He looked around. His heart began pounding as he realized he had stepped directly into a nest of rattlesnakes.

CHAPTER SIX

The rattling noise grew louder, more insistent, and the first of the diamondbacks showed itself to Jacob. Slithering forward from the shadow of the nearby boulder, the three-foot-long reptile reared back, baring its venomous fangs.

He'd heard tell that these snakes were the few that would stand their ground, instead of slither away and hide. Jacob's palms began to sweat, his body on high alert against the death threat.

A second rattlesnake caught his eye, hissing at him from the path straight ahead.

He had only been in the Arizona Territory for a year, not quite long enough that rattlesnake encounters were common for him. Back in Virginia, where he grew up, he knew how to handle the dangerous copperhead or water moccasin, but rattlesnakes were a new threat.

A third and fourth rattlesnake slithered into his view, from underneath the dry shrub in this corner of the canyon. He froze, hand on his revolver, unsure how to proceed.

He knew—he *thought*—the snakes would only come at him if they felt threatened. They probably wouldn't chase him. He froze where he stood, weighing his options. Each second he stayed unmoving was another second Jed Corker could take to get farther away.

More and more of the deadly snakes made themselves heard. The echoing of the rattles became a crescendo, surrounding Jacob. He spun slowly, finding reptiles in all directions alert and warning him of their menace.

Jacob thought back to what he had been taught about rattlesnakes from the locals since arriving in Arizona: that he likely wouldn't be bothered much by them. He hadn't thought to ask what to do in the unlikely event he *was* bothered by them. He hadn't thought it would be so easy to surprise an entire nest of the things. He assumed that he'd been making enough noise to warn them of his approach to let them get away. The animals shouldn't be seeking him out like this.

Something wasn't right here.

Jacob slowly wrapped his fingers around the coil of rope slung over his left shoulder. Grasping it in one hand, he lowered the cord so it was hanging from his fist, nearer to the ground. As one of the snakes made to attack, Jacob used the rope to block the lunge. The rattlesnake's fangs sunk into the rope instead of Jacob's calf.

As the snake shook itself loose, he noticed a disturbance in the dirt around it. Behind the crowd of snakes, there was a trail in the dirt where stones had rolled or slid. They were out of place. The ground here was almost totally flat —why would a stone have moved on its own?

As another snake reared up to hiss at him, Jacob seethed.

This was another trap that Corker had set up for him. Somehow the outlaw had riled up the snakes, putting them on guard—likely after he had already passed the nest and just before Jacob would walk into it. Maybe he tossed a rock or otherwise harassed them out of their burrow, just in time for them to be on the defensive when Jacob made his way through.

He knew he couldn't do anything but wait. There was no going around them, and he couldn't go back. Jacob could only stand still and hope that the mess of rattlers would give up shortly and that Corker wouldn't get too far ahead in the meantime.

Jacob holstered his revolver. Shooting a snake seemed impractical, but his Bowie knife would be a more likely defense in case they did come after him.

As he reached down to his boot, Jacob noticed a stirring out of the corner of his eye. His movement had startled one of the largest rattlesnakes. It lunged forward. Jacob grasped for the hilt of the Bowie knife, but the snake was faster. Before he knew it, the venomous fangs had sunk deep into his right forearm.

Jacob grunted in pain, but managed to wrap his fingers around the knife's handle. In one swift movement, he shook the snake loose and swiped his knife straight across, severing the snake's head from its body before it reached the ground.

He moved the knife to his left hand. He could feel the venom already sinking into his bloodstream. He used the blade to cut back the fabric of his shirt, revealing two small puncture wounds where the fangs had pierced his skin, releasing their deadly defense.

Jacob knew what he had to do—though he had never attempted such a thing.

To his left was a small boulder, about knee-high. With the small bit of strength he still had, Jacob stepped up to the top of it. He would wait out the snakes' fury from here—provided he didn't collapse under the effects of the venom.

He kept his injured arm steady and tried to breathe calm into his thumping heart. Any movement or panic would encourage the blood to pump and send the venom deeper into his bloodstream. With his free hand he patted down his pockets, finally finding what he was looking for in the pocket on his backside: a narrow strip of leather, the strap he had been using to keep his bedroll tied to the saddle. Awkwardly, quickly as he could with one hand, he wrapped the strip around his bicep, tying a clumsy knot and pulling the leather tight with his teeth.

He gasped inadvertently at the pain. The leather cuff cut off his blood circulation even further, but Jacob could feel the effects of the venom already building. He blinked several times in rapid succession, trying to see past the encroaching double vision.

His hand shook as he brought the sharp point of his Bowie knife to his arm. A small X incision at the point of the bite gave him a target, but the pain of it almost made his knees buckle.

With the sleeve clear of the wound, Jacob brought his arm to his mouth and swiftly sucked the venom out. He spat the bloody mouthful to the ground and brought his arm up again. It took four times total for Jacob to feel like he might have gotten as much of the venom out as he could. Losing blood at the same time he was low on water made him lightheaded, but he managed to stay on his feet.

Though the rattling had abated somewhat, Jacob was still surrounded by at least a dozen rattlesnakes, still angry and defending their territory. He moved the knife back to his weakened right hand and pulled his canteen from the strap over his shoulder. After fumbling with the cap, Jacob carefully poured a small bit of water onto his wound.

He hissed at the pain; the water almost burned as it cleaned out the punctures. He didn't have anything to bandage his arm other than the already ripped sleeve, but he couldn't take time to do that as long as he was still surrounded by rattlesnakes.

He felt lightheaded. He must not have gotten all the venom, but he didn't trust himself to try again. Jacob spread his feet apart, trying to balance more evenly on top of the boulder. A wave of nausea crept over him. He fought it as long as he could, then vomited onto the ground before him. The little water he had let himself drink that day now lay in a puddle in the dirt.

The reptiles were beginning to lose interest, and the closer ones recoiled from the liquid splashing in the dirt. Jacob took a deep breath and steeled himself. He couldn't wait all day for the snakes to scatter, but he also couldn't trust himself to get past them in this state.

He stood up straight again, watching the remaining rattlers warily. His knees began to shake a bit, and Jacob knew he couldn't last as he was much longer. Not if his body was going to be able to fight off the infection and trace amounts of venom. He reluctantly opened his canteen and downed most of the remaining water.

If he didn't find more water in the canyon,

he didn't know how he would get himself back to Tucson—with or without the outlaw.

As the last diamondback slithered into its den, Jacob stepped carefully down off the boulder. He looked ahead to the path and for more clues of Corker. The outlaw had succeeded in derailing Jacob's hunt more than once—even injuring him in the process—but he must be running out of tricks.

Just like Jacob was running out of water.

CHAPTER SEVEN

Jacob pulled his canteen off the strap on his shoulder and treated himself to just a single mouthful, nearly emptying the container. His body cried out for water after losing so much sweat in the previous days, and he knew he could only go so much farther without severe repercussions.

He opened and closed his right fist experimentally. Would that small movement send the rattlesnake's venom deeper into his bloodstream? Jacob still felt nauseated and lightheaded. The muscles of his forearm burned around the bite mark, but at this point he didn't seem to be getting any worse. What he mostly needed was a hot meal and rest. Unfortunately, those were the last things he could have right now. If he took one more break, Jed Corker could get away, likely to continue his attacks on innocent people throughout the region.

The path ahead of Jacob was straight and clear—for this section of canyon, at least. He hadn't actually seen another human in days. He usually enjoyed his time in the desert, but this time he was ready to get back. As he continued his pursuit, the bounty hunter remembered the last time he had been so many days into the wilderness.

Back before he left Virginia, he would deliberately take several days away from his land to be alone in the Blue Ridge Mountains. The first couple times, his wife hadn't understood why he wanted to leave her; but as time wore on she began to see how much those days by himself in the wild restored him.

He missed her. And if she had lived through the war and had come west with him, she'd be scolding him something fierce for his negligence on this trail. The difference, of course, was that Jacob could always find water in the Blue Ridge Mountains. Water was everywhere in Virginia. He hadn't thought he would miss it as much as he did at this moment.

Jacob was startled out of his reminiscing by a heavy thudding sound high above him. He looked up swiftly, trying to identify the sound, just in time to see a piece of the canyon wall crumble. A cloud of dirt puffed out where something—a bird? a stone?—hit the jutting-out corner of canyon wall and broke it off. Jacob watched, fascinated, before he grasped what was happening.

As high above him as it was, Jacob hadn't realized just how large the rocky slice of canyon wall was until it was plummeting toward him. Jacob dove to the ground, but it was too little too late. The huge stone crashed into him, jutting hard into his shoulder and ripping his pack from his back, before rolling farther down the canyon.

He groaned into the dirt. That would be another bruise, maybe worse. This hunt was proving to be more physically demanding than he had expected. It would be worth it when he brought in Jed Corker, though.

Jacob rolled onto his back, preparing to get to his feet again, when a panicked thought flashed through his head.

He had rolled onto his back.

He shouldn't be able to roll onto his back.

He should have a canteen strapped there.

He sat up, fully panicked, looking around, and saw his canteen six feet away, where the stone had ripped it from his back, the cap fallen off and the last drops of his water supply dripping into the dirt.

"No!" he exclaimed, scrambling on his knees to the canteen. He caught up the leather bag and was immediately dismayed. There was no weight, no tell-tale sloshing.

The last of his water was gone.

He punched his fist into the dirt in frustration; the pain shot through his already injured arm.

No more water.

He was completely out of water, with who knew how many days of travel in the sun ahead of him, if he couldn't catch Corker soon. This canyon showed signs of foliage, so maybe there was a chance he'd find water. But only a chance. This was the desert, after all.

Now Jacob's best hope was to find Corker and pray the other man still had a supply of water to maintain the both of them.

He pulled himself to his feet and took a deep breath.

If anyone could do this, it was Jacob Payne, bounty hunter.

He began his hike again, deeper into the canyon. The path narrowed ahead, turning slightly to the right. Jacob closed the final steps to meet the unknown around the corner.

CHAPTER EIGHT

Just before he rounded the corner, another familiar scent arrested Jacob's progress. He paused and sniffed again.

For a bounty hunter on the trail in the west, the stench was as common as coffee, and in this case just as welcome. He breathed it in: manure. There was a horse nearby. A horse that would carry him outta here once he'd completed his mission. Like as not, it was Corker's horse, which meant the outlaw himself would also be close.

Jacob crept up around the bend, his back to the wall of the canyon, his hand ready on his revolver to draw if need be. As he peeked around the rock, he spotted the source of the stench.

A dapple gray horse stood near the right wall of the canyon, its reins tied off on the overhanging branch of a mesquite tree. Jacob waited and watched for at least a minute, to be sure, but the horse seemed more or less content. And alone. Its owner was nowhere in sight.

Jacob crept up to the horse, slowly, in case Corker was watching from some unseen location.

"Whoa there, buddy," Jacob said under his breath, one hand outstretched to touch the horse. "You all alone? You okay?" The palm of his hand flat against the horse's neck, Jacob soothed the animal, which had been spooked by his approach.

He looked around, certain he'd find another clue as to the outlaw's whereabouts.

Just a few yards past where the horse stood, the ravine narrowed farther, and huge boulders filled the width of the canyon. The first stood as high as Jacob's chest, and offered no clear path over or around. Jacob could barely picture a man climbing up through the canyon over those rocks, let alone a horse.

When he turned back to Corker's ride, he noticed another reason that the animal had been abandoned here. The tiniest trickle of water dripped down from the crack in the wall of the canyon. There was enough output from this spring to puddle down near Jacob's feet, and he recognized the heel of a boot in the mud leading away, farther up the canyon toward the boulders.

Another clue that Corker had been here.

Jacob grinned to himself. He was closing in. He made a quick plan: He would add some water to his canteen and then continue his hunt. He could leave the horse waiting for when he brought Corker back through the canyon. It wouldn't be long before he found the outlaw's camp. He couldn't go far without his horse, nor could he go away from the only source of water for miles.

After visually searching the canyon again, Jacob reluctantly returned his Bowie knife to the sheathe in his boot and used both hands to maneuver the canteen into place. His left hand was needed to support his weakened right arm.

Once he helped himself to the first few gulps of water, Jacob settled in to fill the canteen for the rest of his hunt. In only a few short minutes, though, he realized he had to change his plan. With such a small output, it would take far too long for Jacob to fill his gallon leather canteen. He elected to fill it halfway now, then again on his way out of the canyon once he had captured Corker. He'd be stopping to claim the horse, and could spend the night in this spot.

He paused for a moment, letting the fresh water course through his system. Even just this small amount was helping. His lightheadedness was clearing and he was feeling more stable on his feet. He could keep moving toward the outlaw.

Once his new water supply was stored away and again strapped over his shoulder, Jacob took a deep breath and assessed the rocks in front of him. This must be where Corker continued up into the canyon, scrambling over boulders, or maybe even squeezing into hiding places between them like the snake he was.

With as much gear as he could carry strapped to his back, Jacob had a slight struggle to climb on top of the first boulder. He almost lost his hat when he had to bend so far forward to get a solid grip on the rock. His right arm around the snakebite twinged, but he didn't let that stop him.

The sole of his boot skidded only once on the smooth surface of stone. When Jacob reached the top of the first boulder, he stood upright and surveyed the path before him. Ahead were more boulders to climb over, but there seemed to be another stretch of clear ground in about ten yards. If he could keep his feet under him, he'd be up the canyon in just a couple minutes.

He felt something cool fall on his hand and immediately looked up for a bird or plant on the cliff above. No movement caught his eye. There was no signal as to what had dropped on him, until Jacob noticed the blue sky above was gone. He had gotten used to the lack of sun, being deep in the canyon for so long, but when he looked up he realized that a thick gray cloud covered the sky at the top of the ravine.

The storm he had been warned about had arrived. Raindrops fell slowly at first, peppering his sleeves with wet spots here and there.

Jacob laughed out loud, his chuckle echoing against the walls.

Water. It was water. For as many days as he had been looking for water, for as careful as he had been to not run out of it early and not put himself in danger, now it was raining.

And right after he had found a spring.

Rain in the desert.

Jacob lifted his face to the sky. Cool drops of water the size of silver dollars dropped gently on his face. He closed his eyes and opened his mouth, letting the water fall over him. He leaned so far back, his hat fell completely off this time. He caught it but let the cool rain stream down over his head and his hair and down to his collar.

The rain started to fall heavily.

Then, Jacob heard the bone-shaking crack of thunder.

CHAPTER NINE

Thunder rolled through the canyon. Jacob felt it in his bones. Lightning flashed, another crack of thunder following only two seconds later. The storm had closed in on him before he'd realized it was coming. How had he missed it? Wind whipped around him, racing though the canyon. He slammed his hand to his head, holding his hat in place. Being this deep in the canyon, surrounded by stone walls on all sides, Jacob hadn't even noticed the drop in temperature or the increased humidity.

All thought of capturing Corker was forgotten while Jacob prioritized what he needed to do to prepare for the coming downpour. He holstered his revolver, protecting it from the wet as much as he could.

Lightning flashed again, the thunder rumble immediately following. This storm—monsoon, they called it here—was right on top of him. He had no chance to find shelter and would have to ride out the rain as best he could.

The boulder under his feet was beginning to get slick with water. The sole of his boot slipped again and Jacob stumbled a little to keep his balance. Where could he move? If he climbed down again, he'd be stuck in the mud as more rain fell. But could he climb up to the next higher boulder with all the slickness? Should he even attempt it?

The rain came faster now, thicker, obscuring his sight. Jacob used the back of his hand to wipe the water from his eyes, blinking rapidly. The brim of his hat couldn't stop the sheet of water falling from the sky. The rope coiled around his shoulder began to feel heavier as it soaked through.

His foot glided over the surface of the boulder, and this time he wasn't able to regain his balance under the weight and strength of the relentless rain. The boot slid forward and out from under him, and as Jacob fell his lower back smashed against the boulder he had just been standing on.

"Argh!" he cried, the pain surprising him. Jacob arched his back, landing hard on the pack of supplies and just keeping his head from also cracking on the rock. As he tumbled, he felt the muscle on his back bruise almost immediately. He crumpled to the now-muddy ground at the foot of the boulder, water rising around him.

In what had been the simple pursuit of an outlaw, Jacob had been battered from all sides and now ached all over. The water rushed down over the boulders, pouring over him where he lay on the ground. While his hat kept the water off his face for the moment, every other inch of Jacob was soaked. The ground beneath him softened into mud quickly, his weight sinking deeper every second. He braced himself against the side of the boulder, struggling to pull himself to standing under the sheer strength of the water now pouring onto him from the flow over the rocks.

He had never seen a flash flood. The mellow hills of Virginia spread out any influx of rain, the many rivers and creeks quickly draining into the Atlantic Ocean. Even the strongest storms weren't enough to fill a Virginian valley this quickly. But the focused narrowness of this canyon, the hard rock that denied any absorption, directed the full downpour straight toward Jacob.

Somewhere farther upstream, Jed Corker must have been barely hanging on himself.

Jacob couldn't keep his feet under him in this current. He couldn't afford to lose any ground or time. He needed to anchor himself and find a way to hold his own so he could cross this flood and get farther up the canyon to nab his target.

He looked up the canyon, blinking into the sheet of water, past the boulder he had just fallen from, and spied the nearly petrified stump of a tree. It was at least twenty feet up the canyon, across the quickly forming river rushing down toward him. That was it. His anchor. A tree that size should have deep, strong roots, and if Jacob could get a solid grip, he could wait out the storm holding tight to that.

He pulled his hat down farther on his head, tight, praying it wouldn't blow off while his hands were otherwise busy. The rope was soaked through, its weight digging into his shoulder. He hadn't yet had much practice tying slip knots and lassoing, but he would have to make it work.

The first knot fell apart completely. Jacob's fingers must have slipped in the rain; he hadn't made the loops correctly, or he didn't pull the rope tight enough. He wasn't sure where he went wrong, so he shook it apart and started over. He bent forward a little more to keep the rain out of his face, but the water pouring off the brim of his hat formed a veritable curtain around him.

"Drat," he muttered under his breath, and started again.

He tied the loose knot, pulled the end through, paused to shake more rain out of his face, tightened it, and finished up his lasso.

He took a deep breath and looked for the tree again, almost falling under the pour of rain. The thick clouds rolling in had completely obscured the sun, and the heavy shadows made it difficult to see too far in front of him.

Jacob could almost laugh. All them Tucson locals had been right to warn him.

A flash of lightning brightened the ravine for a split second and Jacob spied his target. Swinging the rope above his head, Jacob winced at the pain in his arm. He needed to put more effort and power behind it to counter the downpour.

His first throw was short, so he hurried to pull the rope back toward him.

He tried again, fighting through the pain and the rain to swing the rope above his head and propel it toward the tree. He held his breath for the two seconds before the loop landed over the top of the stump.

Jacob grasped the rope with both hands and pulled hard. The rope tightened around the stump.

He had his anchor. Now he just had to pull himself to it.

Jacob could barely hang on to the rope in this torrent. The coarse, wet fiber cut into his hands. How would he keep moving up the canyon? The longer he struggled, the longer Corker had to get away.

CHAPTER TEN

No sooner had Jacob secured his rope around the tree stump than lightning flashed, thunder rolled, and the storm intensified yet again. The current of water filling the canyon continued to rise at an alarming rate.

This was the flash flood he had been warned about.

Just as he took his first step back up onto the wet boulder, he lost his footing. Holding on to the rope, he found himself being swung this way and that in the flow, his body slamming into the boulder. After a few hard crashes against the rock, Jacob got his body pointing the right direction and, both hands on the rope, planted the soles of his boots against the side of the boulder.

Hand over hand, Jacob clung tightly to his rope, step by step up the side of the boulder. The water, combined with the thread of the rope, began wearing down the skin of his hands. His palms burned, and as the water below him pulled his body in every direction, the tugging and rubbing on his hands wore through. He couldn't tell if water or blood was dripping down his wrist, or both. But still he held on.

With the help of the rope, Jacob climbed back up the boulder. His boots slipped over and over again, unable to get purchase under the rushing water, but he managed to pull himself up.

Strength. Willpower. Adrenaline.

He needed to keep moving, to keep pursuing his target. His right forearm still ached, but still he held on.

Once he reached the top of the boulder again, he didn't linger. Jacob wrapped the rope more securely around his wrist and stepped off the high point and into the water on the other side.

The current crushed his body against the rock, but he was determined. He couldn't even feel the ground under his feet, but he used his arms to pull himself forward, farther up the rope, closer to the tree stump that would be his safe haven.

Jacob risked a look up the canyon to see how far he still had to go, but almost immediately he had to lower his head again. He let go of the rope with one hand to clamp his hat to his head. If he lost that, he'd have a long, hot travel back to Tucson with no shade from the sun.

There were three more sizable boulders between Jacob and his end goal. Three more places he could be smashed and bounced around in the current. He kept moving. Hand over hand, palm slick with water and blood, his fingers cramping in their death grip.

Another man might have given up long ago, but not Jacob Payne. Every foot closer to the outlaw was progress, and he would not let himself rest. Forward along his drenched rope he went, until he finally climbed up to the petrified tree stump sitting above the waterline on the side of the canyon.

Jacob closed his eyes and wrapped the rope around his arm, and his arm around the tree, to secure himself. Water gushed toward him from all directions. Rain still burst from the sky, while more streams spilled off the canyon wall next to him, splashing onto his hat brim and shoulders. The floodwaters rushing over the boulders were as high as his knees now.

Under the roar of the storm, Jacob started laughing. He couldn't even hear himself, but he couldn't help but laugh, a full-throated laugh up into the storm-drenched sky. After three days of struggling and rationing, when every thought was of making his water supply last as long as possible, now the water was his biggest threat. Now all he wanted was for the water to stop.

As he laughed, Jacob thought he heard another laugh from elsewhere in the canyon, before he realized it was his own laughter's echo.

He could hear it. He could hear himself again.

He looked up to the sky, blinking against the falling rain, and realized the clouds were moving on. The storm was abating. There was no telling when the floodwaters would fully subside, but at least Jacob knew there wouldn't be more water.

Jacob fished his nearly empty canteen from the strap on his back and bent to refill it from the flash flood still rushing over his ankles. The added weight on his own back instead of a horse's might slow him down, but having enough water for his journey back was worth it.

Jacob took one last drink of water before he went on. He pulled his rope from the tree stump, still knotted, and coiled it in a loop to drape over his shoulder.

His gaze scanned the surface of the water as the flood receded. The storm had likely washed away all of Corker's trail, so he would have to start all over again. But that wouldn't be any trouble. If Corker moved, if Corker even breathed, Jacob would know it, and he would find him. There was only one direction he could be.

Jacob secured his canteen over his shoulder again and jumped down from his ledge into the ankle-deep water. It splashed around his boots as he took the first few tentative steps in the muddy path.

Jacob began running up the canyon. Now that he was past the boulders the ground had only a slight incline, and he made quick progress. He would catch up with Corker and surprise the man before he had even realized the storm had passed.

The ravine curved again around to the left a few yards ahead. As he ran around the bend,

Jacob spotted movement—something dark gray and out of place—to the far right up ahead. He paused, hand reflexively on his gun. The thing was bobbing slightly, and as he crept closer Jacob realized what it was—a Stetson.

Corker had lost his hat, the idiot.

Jacob left it where it was; he might let the outlaw retrieve it once he'd been subdued, but for now it simply served as a confirmation that Jacob was close. He was on the murderer's trail and would soon bring this chase to a close.

He may have thrown all manner of obstacles at the bounty hunter, but like many outlaws, Corker had underestimated him to his downfall.

After he passed the outlaw's hat sinking in the mud, Jacob slowed his advance. Corker would be close, and he didn't want to come upon the murderer unawares. The man had already tried to shake his trail several times and had attempted to kill him several more. There was every reason to suspect he'd be waiting for the bounty hunter in ambush. He was dangerous and unstable, and Jacob would need every advantage to take him in to meet justice.

The canyon narrowed ahead of him and Jacob couldn't see beyond the tight passageway. He paused and took a deep breath, readying himself for battle. The floodwaters had completely abated, leaving just mud underfoot. He lowered his coil of rope and pack of supplies to the ground, lightening his load and making himself more limber for whatever Corker had waiting for him.

Jacob needed to know what waited for him beyond the bend. He doubled back to pick up Corker's hat and sidled flat along the side of the canyon. At the turn in the passageway, he decided on a quick experiment: he held out Corker's hat into view.

One revealing crack after another sounded, echoing around the stone, as three rapid gunshots pierced the brim of the dark gray Stetson. Jacob pulled the prop back before his hand got blown off.

It was an ambush, just as he suspected. Corker was just the sort of man who would get the jump on another, murdering innocent bank tellers and now shooting at what he thought was Jacob without warning.

Jacob always preferred to take in his targets alive, but if Corker wanted a fight, he would get one.

Jacob thought back, counting. That was three shots at the hat, and another at Paint at the start of the canyon. If he hadn't reloaded, Corker only had a couple shots left. Jacob would have to press his advantage quickly, before the other man rearmed himself. He stayed completely still, not making a sound to give away his presence. For all the outlaw knew, he had hit and killed the lawman trailing him.

Jacob listened as hard as he could around the turn in the canyon. The shuffle of footsteps told him Corker was only a few yards away. He reached down to arm himself with the Bowie knife from his boot. He was not a man to kill if he didn't have to. Whatever he found around the bend, Jacob wouldn't be shooting the other man in the back.

More sounds of feet moving back and forth, and Jacob thought Corker sounded anxious, unsteady. That meant he'd probably be on alert and waiting for Jacob. He'd have to wait it out and give the outlaw time to let down his guard.

Jacob pressed his back to the stone wall and breathed as shallowly as he could. He'd wait forever if need be. He waited so long his pants had begun to dry from the flood. If there was one advantage Jacob had over most outlaws, it was patience. These wild men with their need for immediate gratification—robbing a bank instead of earning an honest living—could never out-wait the bounty hunter.

After an untold period of time, Corker had

been quiet long enough that Jacob felt that the other man had the advantage. Whatever sounds Jacob's first movement made would give him away, so he'd have to take Corker in one swift movement.

In one long step, Jacob was around the bend in the canyon and facing Jed Corker. The outlaw, lanky with stringy blond hair hanging limply around his face, was leaning against the canyon wall, gun in hand, but stood up straight when he saw the bounty hunter.

"Hands up, Corker," Jacob cried.

The outlaw chuckled and shot. Jacob saw the movement and ducked back behind the cover of rock just in time. One more shot down. He was close to being able to overpower Corker.

"You don't have a chance, boy," he said, coming back around the rock. He stalked toward Corker, a weapon in each hand.

Corker aimed again, but Jacob didn't have time to take cover. The gun jammed and the outlaw cursed his luck while frantically trying shake something lose. Jacob grinned. He had seen it before. Men like this who thought they were invincible never took the time on basic things like gun cleaning.

He took several steps forward, aiming to take down Corker while he was distracted, but the other man looked up at the last second. He raised his revolver above his head, bringing it down toward Jacob's temple.

Bowie knife in his left hand, Jacob swiped at Corker, slicing the man across the wrist and deep into the meaty flesh of his thumb. The outlaw cried out in pain, dropping his gun in the process. Jacob wasted no time in kicking the weapon across the canyon floor and thrusting his own revolver at Corker.

"Hands in the air, you devil," Jacob said in a low, threatening tone.

The outlaw glowered at Jacob as he raised his hands in surrender, blood dripping down and staining his sleeve.

CHAPTER TWELVE

"That's right, Corker," Jacob said, pointing his revolver at the outlaw's chest. "Nice and slow, and maybe you'll live to see another day."

Once he was sure there would be no sudden moves, Jacob sheathed his Bowie knife and picked up Corker's pistol from the dirt at his feet. The knife went back in his boot and the gun went in his holster, while his own revolver stayed in his hand.

"Move. Now."

He gestured with the gun, and Corker shuffled forward a couple steps back up the ravine toward the narrow passageway. His hat lay in the mud where Jacob had left it.

"Pick it up," Jacob commanded.

He didn't take his eyes off the outlaw, tense

and ready for any attempt at escape, while he bent down to retrieve his Stetson. Sitting just a few feet farther was the coil of rope and supplies Jacob had left behind. With the gun trained on the outlaw, Jacob used one foot, stuck it under the coil, and lifted his leg just high enough to be able to grab the rope without bending down and leaving himself vulnerable to the other man.

Corker glared at him.

"Hands in the air, I said."

Corker spat at Jacob; the glob of phlegm landed only inches from Jacob's feet, but he raised his hands again, high above his head.

"Now," Jacob said calmly. "Pick up this pack."

Corker glared but complied.

Jacob continued, "I'm gonna come over there and I'm gonna tie this rope around your wrists. You best not do anything stupid, now."

Corker didn't respond, but slowly lowered his hands. The two men eyed each other as the armed bounty hunter slowly, cautiously made his way across the several feet between them.

The look in the bank robber's eye made Jacob wary. He didn't trust this man as far as he could spit. Sure enough, as soon as Jacob got close enough, Corker kicked up his leg, aiming to disarm him. In a flash, Jacob fired the revolver. At this close range he hit exactly where he was aiming. Corker's left sleeve darkened in a bloom of blood where the bullet hit its mark.

"You—" Corker's litany of cursing was lost among his groans of pain.

"Can't say I didn't warn you."

With Corker so distracted, Jacob easily subdued him and bound his wrists together, further wrapping the rope tightly around the other man's arms. Corker yelped as Jacob pulled the knot tight.

"That'll have to do you for a bandage till we get somewhere," Jacob said. "I suggest you don't delay our travelin' any more than you have to."

With the tail end of the rope in one hand and his revolver in the other, Jacob had successfully protected the citizens of neighboring towns from this godless outlaw.

"Move," Jacob said, gesturing toward the mouth of the canyon with his gun.

Corker glared at him. For several breathless seconds, Jacob wasn't sure the captive would obey.

"I really prefer to take you alive," Jacob said casually. "But I don't particularly have to."

Corker heaved a giant sigh and turned to lead the way out of the canyon. He had a bit of trouble climbing over the high boulders with his wrists tied, but Jacob let him take as long as he needed.

When they reached the outlaw's horse, Corker sidled on up to the animal's side as if to make it known it was his property.

Jacob tied the end of the rope to the saddle, securing the knot and tugging experimentally.

"You ain't riding my horse," Corker griped.

"I sure as shootin' am," Jacob replied. "You shouldn'ta killt my horse if you didn't want me to take yours. Besides, the way I hear it, you stole this horse and it ain't yours anyway."

Using the barrel of his revolver, he gestured again at where he wanted Corker to go.

"You walk on ahead, now. I'll not be turning my back to you or untying you at any point. I know your tricks now, Corker, and you'll not be slipping away from me this time."

Corker called him all manner of names under his breath as he shuffled on ahead.

Jacob watched him carefully as he mounted the dapple gray and began the walk back to the mouth of the canyon. Corker dragged his feet, but a periodic poke in the back with the toe of his boot and Jacob had him moving again.

Valleseco was closer than Tucson, only about a day's ride from where they were in the desert. He'd take Corker there and let the bank and the sheriff decide what to do with him. They had two full canteens of water and at least three hours of daylight left before they needed to make camp. Jacob ignored the outlaw's complaining and kept his eyes looking up—up toward the sun, and toward the lawmen they'd meet the next day.

<u>**Jacob Payne Series:**</u>

<u>*Trouble By Any Name*</u>

Danger in the Canyon

Justice for Jasper

Blood on the Mountain

Outlaw Country

Death By Grit

<u>*Desert Rage*</u>

<u>*Arizona Legacy*</u>

<u>*Fool's Demise*</u>

<u>*Silent Night*</u>

<u>*Jacob Payne Box Set: Books 1-3*</u>

<u>*Jacob Payne Box Set: Books 4-6*</u>

<u>*Jacob Payne Box Set: Books 7-9*</u>

<u>**Courage On The Oregon Trail Series:**</u>

<u>*Westward Courage*</u>

<u>*Faithful Trail*</u>

<u>*Frontier Sisters*</u>

<u>**Other Western Novels by A.T. Butler:**</u>

<u>*Hawke's Revenge*</u>

<u>*Loyalty's Price*</u>

Jacob Payne almost got himself bit.

"Whoa, there!" He pulled his fingers away just in time. The dapple gray mustang had seemed friendly enough, but as soon as Jacob's fingers brushed close to its mouth, it snapped at him. Jacob glared at the horse's current owner. "Thought you said this one was broken."

Caleb Shaw widened his eyes, wearing his most innocent expression. "He is. You musta riled him somehow."

"Uh huh," Jacob muttered.

He turned back to examine the horse, keeping out of reach of its strong jaw—which was no way to really learn anything, but he kept trying. Jacob needed to have something to ride out of there today.

The bounty hunter's previous horse, Paint, had been shot from under him while he was on the trail of a bank robber out in the desert. In the several days since he captured Jed Corker and turned him over to the lawful authorities, he had managed to do without a horse of his own, staying in town and going everywhere on foot.

But now, looking at Shaw's meager selection, Jacob wondered how much longer he could do without. It's not that he couldn't afford a fine horse, but more that there were none to be had. His current options were a mare that had given birth two days earlier, a Morgan that could not be younger than twenty years, or this one with the biting—Shaw called him Smoke. Jacob wondered how he'd manage to bridle the creature without losing his fingers.

"You sure you don't have any others for sale, Shaw?" Jacob asked, turning back to the the man.

"Payne, I swear—"

"Jacob Payne!" a big voice shouted from the doorway of the livery. "Anyone seen Payne?"

"Who's asking?" Jacob shouted back. Shielding his eyes against the sunny backdrop, Jacob made out the silhouette of a tall, thin man walking toward him. Out here in Arizona Territory, a stranger knowing his name could either be very good or very bad.

"U.S. Marshal Owen Santos," the man said as he approached.

As the stranger got closer, Jacob noticed he was holding up a badge. From this distance he couldn't make out what the badge said, but he'd heard of Santos all right.

"I'm Jacob Payne. What can I do for you, Marshal?"

Santos took off his hat and offered his hand to the bounty hunter. The Marshal stood taller than Jacob by several inches, which was uncommon, but was leaner than a bean pole. Jacob's broad shoulders could probably hide the other man behind him twice over.

He shook the marshal's hand, then noticed Shaw awkwardly watching the interaction.

"Have you met Caleb Shaw, Marshal?" he asked, gesturing.

The lawman glanced at the livery owner, barely acknowledging him before turning his attention back to Jacob. "I'm gonna tell you this straight. I need your help. I can legally force you into helping, but I'd rather you come willingly."

Jacob was half defensive and half amused by this approach. Though he wasn't technically a man of the law, he still respected what men like Santos had to do. "What is it you need, sir?"

Santos let out a deep sigh and rolled his eyes. His annoyance rolled off of him in waves. "Well, seems the sheriff down in Jasper can't do the job he was elected to do. He's called on the marshal's office for assistance, and all my men are out in the field."

"Assistance with what?"

"Claims he's identified a wanted murderer, one Floyd Daly. But seeing as the man is currently in the employ of the Rockville Mining Company, he's having a devil of a time even getting close to him."

"You need me to go down and capture this Daly character?"

"Oh, I don't mind goin' down there to collect the man myself, but I don't dare trust the sheriff to back me up if I need it. I need a capable associate by my side if things go south. You're the first person I thought of."

"Why me?"

"All I been hearin' these last few months is 'Jacob Payne *this*' and 'Jacob Payne *that*.' You've made quite the impression since you arrived in

Arizona. Bonnie, in particular, seems to like the taste of your name in her mouth."

Jacob smiled. Bonnie, his favorite waitress at the San Xavier Cafe just a few blocks away, sure did make his visits to Tucson pleasant. But she couldn't be the only one talking about him to the U.S. Marshal. Likely the sheriffs of Bennettsville or Valleseco—or maybe even San Adrian, if they had a new sheriff already—would be speaking well of him.

"I'm happy to help if I can, Marshal."

"Much obliged. I'll deputize you now and we'll be on our way tomorrow morning."

"One problem, sir. I still don't have a horse—"

"Since Jed Corker shot yours? Yeah, I heard about that, too. Hanging's too good for that one, I tell you. Well, fine." Santos looked around the stable for the first time. "None of these?"

Jacob hesitated. "I was hoping to be able to invest in a more reliable animal."

Santos nodded. "I see." He glared at Caleb. "Well, in that case, just leave it to me. I'll find a mount for you by tomorrow. You can't get the thing killed, though."

"I'll do my best," Jacob said with a grin. "You

have any idea why the sheriff down in Jasper can't get his man?"

Santos sighed. "Like I said—Daly managed to get a job working at the Vernon Copper Mine and has apparently made himself indispensable. The boss always has some excuse why he can't be bothered or why they can't reveal his whereabouts."

"All right." Jacob considered what kind of security might be around a mine. "We'll find a way to get to him."

"Damn right, we will," Santos said vehemently. "Glad you'll be joining me, Payne. Come on over to my office. We got a lot to do."

He led the way out of the livery.

"So you won't be taking Smoke?" Caleb asked before Jacob left.

The bounty hunter looked at the other man, exasperated. "The horse that almost *bit* me? No, Caleb. Not this time."

Caleb nodded, while Jacob hurried to catch up with Santos and prepare to track down the outlaw Daly.

ABOUT THE AUTHOR

I grew up in the southwest—California Missions, snakes and constant threat of drought weaving the backdrop of my childhood.

But it wasn't until I moved to Texas a few years ago that the magic and mythology of the American West began to seep into my soul.

I'd love to write about Jacob Payne for a long time. ...

If you enjoyed this book, a review on your favorite retailer would be greatly appreciated.

Be sure to sign up for my newsletter for all the updates on future books.

- A

www.ingramcontent.com/pod-product-compliance
Lightning Source LLC
Chambersburg PA
CBHW032042180726
48284CB00008B/2713